Ready for School

Written by
Stephen Rickard

Illustrated by
Dawn Clarke

On Monday, Kim went to school —
but she forgot her pencil.

She went to school on Tuesday.
She took her pencil –
but she forgot her coat.

On Wednesday,
Kim took her pencil
and her coat
to school –
but she forgot her hat.

She took her pencil,
her coat
and her hat
to school on Thursday –
but she forgot her ruler.

On Friday
Kim went to school.
She took her pencil
and her coat,
her hat
and her ruler –
but she forgot her lunchbox.

On Saturday Kim got up.
She took her pencil
and her coat,
her hat, her lunchbox
and her ruler.
"No school today!"
said Mum.